PB MET J

Written By
KATELYN ARONSON

Illustrated By
SARAH REBAR

VIKING

VIKING
An imprint of Penguin Random House LLC, New York

First published in the United States of America by Viking,
an imprint of Penguin Random House LLC, 2023

Text copyright © 2023 by Katelyn Aronson
Illustrations copyright © 2023 by Sarah Rebar

Visit us online at penguinrandomhouse.com.

Library of Congress Cataloging-in-Publication Data is available.

Manufactured in China

ISBN 9780593327395

1 3 5 7 9 10 8 6 4 2

HH

Design by Opal Roengchai
Text set in ITC Avant Garde Gothic Std and Hank BT Roman
The illustrations in this book were created digitally

For Sandra F., after all these years. —K. A.

To Mom, for encouraging all my drawing and reading!
And for always making the best PB&Js. —S. R.

Once upon a kitchen,
the Fridgers chilled on one side.
The Cupboard Crew loafed
about on the other.

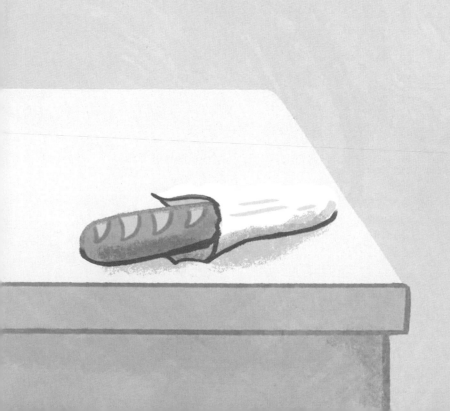

Across the way, it was the same sour grapes.

Aw, nuts, thought Peanut Butter.
Can the Fridgers be that bad?
He had a secret question he'd always
wanted to ask a Fridger . . .

The Friday Night Jam was the only time the Fridgers and the Cupboard Crew mingled on the island in between.

Tonight they'd gathered as usual,
determined to out-dance one another.
Jars shimmied, spun, and twirled across
the countertop.

Peanut Butter sighed. He wasn't the best at boogying.
He couldn't help but notice how Jelly excelled at twirling, though.
She looked a lot sweeter than the average Fridger, too.
He might just get close enough to ask his secret question
once and for all . . .

"Ahem . . . You're from the fridge, right?"

"Yes. I'm Jelly—*J* for short."

"I'm Peanut Butter. Er . . . *PB* for short!"

They got to talking, and J didn't seem cold to PB at all. Plus, she smelled like berries. Sure, J found PB a little nutty, but he asked interesting questions . . .

"Speaking of the fridge," PB said, "It looks so cool and glowy inside. What happens when the door . . ."

J blushed.

PB couldn't believe that fancy-pants Pickles.

How dare he interrupt!

I guess Fridgers only talk with Fridgers, PB thought.

He wished he'd never come.

He headed home to the cupboard.

That's when things spun out of control . . .

Jelly took a twirl for the worst and
completely lost her lid.
The eggs quit rocking and rolling.
The slicer stopped strumming. The jars froze.
Everyone knew what was coming next . . .

KLING

KLING-ITY

KLANG!

"DOG!" they gasped.

SNIFF SNIFF. The dog caught a whiff of berries.

SNIFF SNIFF. Now his paws were on the counter.

Jelly's glass jar rattled.

"Aw, nuts!" PB watched the awful scene from up in the cupboard.
There was only one thing to do.
And only he could do it.
PB jumped . . .

. . . and landed—*WHAM!*—on the dog's tail . . .
ARF! ARF! ARF! ARF!

The poor pooch forgot about Jelly,
but PB lay on the floor, lidless.
His peanutty perfume
drifted until . . .

"Jeepers! PB!" cried Jelly.
There was only one thing to do.
And only she could do it.
"EVERYONE!" Jelly commanded.
"LID LAUNCH!"

The condiments sprang into action.
They popped their tops, undid their lids,
and catapulted their caps into the air.

Footsteps sounded on the stairs.

"BAD DOG!" came a voice.

During kitchen cleanup, tops were swapped.
Lids were switched.
The Cupboard Crew got mixed up
with the Fridgers.

Milk and Hot Cocoa hit it off pretty well.
Pickles found himself overheating in
the cupboard, but didn't have
the courage to climb down.
As for PB . . .

Suddenly, PB remembered the secret question he'd always wanted to ask.

From now on, we all stick together!

Hey, everyone! What happens when the door closes?

The fridge door swung shut
and out went the light.